THE GIFT

LESLEY DRANE

This book is dedicated to my mum, my most ardent fan

ACKNOWLEDGEMENTS

I would like to thank Gillian Manning and John Guilfoyle for their critique and editing, and for keeping me on the right path.

Thanks to Red Cape Publishing for their expertise, advice and formatting.

Cover design by Charlotte@giftsbycharlotte.com

Cabin illustration by Charlotte@giftsbycharlotte.com

The Gift

It was just after 3 pm. Elinor was peeling spuds at the kitchen sink when she heard the knocker rat-a-tat on the wooden door of her cottage. Putting down the potato and peeler, she rinsed her hands and dried them. Elinor opened her front door and thought Christmas had come early. The guy at the door was so tall, her first view of him was of his broad chest and slim hips. Stepping back, she looked up to see his face and wasn't disappointed. A handsome man, with grey eyes, an aquiline nose and, a generous mouth smiled at her. Elinor licked her lips.

The devil on her shoulder whispered into her ear. *"Elinor, you must get his phone number."*

Common sense arrived though, pushing the imp off his perch and said, *"Behave Elinor, and act your age."* With the sun shining on his shaven head, giving the appearance of a halo, Elinor grinned at him.

The man asked Elinor to confirm her name as he had a delivery for her. This surprised her as she hadn't ordered anything off Amazon, and wasn't expecting a supermarket delivery either. She asked him what he had for her.

"A cabinet," he replied. "From Delhi. It was sent by sea from a Mrs. Gertrude Wilson."

He offered to bring it into the cottage for her. Elinor gratefully accepted and asked him if he would like a mug of tea or coffee, hoping that he would stay a while.

"Black coffee with one sugar please, and thank you. My name is Jimmy by the way," he replied. Elinor went to the kitchen to make his drink plus a white coffee for herself, whilst Jimmy disappeared to the van to pick up the cabinet.

"Where do you want this?" he asked, as he reappeared through the front door. "It would sit quite nicely in your hall, I think?" Elinor agreed, so that's where he put it and stood back to admire it. Made of antique rosewood, about three feet long and two and a half feet high, it stood on four clawed feet; with a hinged lid and a lock set into the wood at the front. Two panels were below the lid, across the front with one on either side, with markings. At either edge of the cabinet was a set of protruding small drawers, all with matching brass knobs. Along the top of the lid and the front of the cabinet, etchings were engraved into the rosewood. It was a magnificent piece of furniture. As Jimmy studied it, the cabinet gave the impression that it was settling itself into position, seemingly making itself at home.

Elinor returned with two mugs and set them down on the dining table. Walking over to Jimmy, she too studied the cabinet and wondered out loud how long it would stay put. He gave her a strange look and she explained that up to now the cabinet had always ended up back at the antiquity shop, no matter where it had been sent. This sent a shudder down his spine! "And yet you still purchased it?" he asked, surprised that Elinor wanted it.

Elinor explained that she had seen it in an

antiquity store in Delhi some time ago and had fallen in love with it, but wasn't able to bring it home on the plane. She had been with her Aunt Gertrude at the time and they had chatted to Vihaan, the owner of the store.

"He told me that the cabinet had been in his shop for a long time. He had sold it many times over the years, but each time it reappeared in his shop, obviously waiting for the right person to claim it. Gertrude must have gone back to the store after I returned home. I wasn't aware she was sending it to me, she never said a word! She is a lovely aunt, and has bought it as a gift for me, but not told me in case it didn't turn up. I must ring her and let her know that it has arrived."

Jimmy laughed. "You might want to wait a few days before you do that, just in case it, um, vanishes! I don't suppose you have a key for the lock?" Elinor just chuckled.

"Come and have your coffee before it gets cold," she picked up her mug and continued, "My aunt asked Vihaan, the shop owner, the same question regarding the lock, and do you know what he replied? 'The cabinet holds many secrets, Gertrude,' he obviously knows her. 'The person who the cabinet chooses to stay with will have no problem with the lock.' So I can only guess that either the lock will just open or I will find the key." Jimmy sipped at his drink and turned in his seat to have another look at the cupboard. He hadn't had any difficulty picking it up to bring it in, although it looked substantial and heavy. He pushed his chair back and got up, walked over to the cabinet, and went to pick it up again, but this time he found that he couldn't; it appeared to be set into the hardwood floor. He looked at Elinor.

"That is certainly one strange item of furniture, I had no trouble putting it in the van, nor taking it back out, but I cannot for the life of me pick it up now!"

"In that case, maybe it is here to stay. How amazing if it has chosen me to be its final owner. Do you live far from here? You are welcome to stay for dinner; I was peeling potatoes when you knocked, intending to make a cottage pie. Once the spuds have cooked it won't take long in the oven." Elinor was shocked at the words that spilled out of her mouth; she hadn't intended to invite a complete stranger to dinner.

"Oh, that sounds great, I'm starving, didn't have time for lunch today, and no, I don't live far, only five miles or so from here. You were my last call. Oh, and call me Jim."

Elinor had surprised Jim with the invite, but he had to admit that Elinor seemed an attractive woman, maybe a bit older than him, but what the hell, you only live once!

Jim said he'd go home, park up the van, freshen up and come back later in his car.

"I will be about an hour, is that OK?"

"Yes, dinner will be ready by then."

As he left, she wondered if he would come back; perhaps she had frightened him off by her invitation to dinner—ah well, I will find out soon enough, she thought. She got busy finishing the potatoes and put them in a saucepan, filled it with hot water from the kettle, and left them on the hob to cook. Meanwhile, she wanted a closer look at the cabinet.

The cabinet had made itself at home, the claws giving the impression that they had spread a little; it seemed slightly shorter since Jim had set it down. She stroked the top of the lid, feeling the etching in the rosewood. The wood seemed to glow where the sunlight from the window caught it. Leaning down to inspect the lock, she pressed her forefinger against it and tried to open the lid. The lid remained firmly closed. Elinor checked the time with the clock that hung above the cupboard and calculated the four and a half hour time difference between the UK and Delhi. About 8.30 pm where her aunt lived. She would ring Gertrude and thank her for the beautiful gift.

Picking up the landline phone and dialling her aunt's number, she waited for it to connect and her aunt to pick up. She didn't wait long.

"Hi Gertrude, how are you?"

"Hello my darling, I'm fine. I was just thinking about you. Has the cabinet that you coveted so much arrived?" Elinor looked towards the piece of furniture and smiled.

"Yes, about an hour ago. It looks set to stay. That was so kind of you, thank you so much. I love it!"

Her aunt laughed, "Anything for my favourite niece! Vihaan organised it, he wouldn't even let me pay for it. He is a lovely man you know, I care for him a lot," and sighed down the phone.

Thinking of Jim, Elinor suggested, "Well, you could ask him to dinner, why not? Women don't need to wait for the men to ask you know! Besides which, you will have to contact him to let him know that the cabinet has arrived intact and seems to have made itself at home." Gertrude's laugh tinkled in her ear.

"That is a really good idea, why didn't I think of that? Am only seventy, plenty of life in this old dog yet! I will ring him right now! I'll speak to you later in the week and let you know how it went. Bye darling, talk soon." The line went dead before Elinor had a chance to reply or ask about the lock. Chuckling, she set the phone back on its base.

Prodding the potatoes with a fork and finding them ready to mash, she drained them, tossed them back in the saucepan, added butter, a little milk, and pepper, and set about mashing them. Retrieving the casserole dish from the fridge with the meat already cooked from earlier, added the mash on top. Checking the oven, she opened the door and set the dish on the shelf and, closed the door. Setting the timer for 30 minutes, Elinor went to the bathroom to freshen up.

The cabinet was satisfied with its place under the ticking clock and the old oak beams; with the sunlight still shining on its lid, it glowed quietly. Maybe it would open its lock later and reveal its contents; movement could be heard inside. It would wait just a bit longer…

Jim knocked on the door and looked at the view whilst he waited for Elinor to open it. The sixteenth century thatched cottage had been built right by the sea; the water sparkling in the sunlight. The land rose up from the sand keeping the cottage safe from the incoming tide. With the sea air making him feel hungry, he was looking forward to the meal. He had a bottle of wine and a bottle of soda water with him. The wine was for Elinor and the soda water for himself as he didn't drink and drive. He lived inland so couldn't see the sea from his flat and reflected that Elinor must enjoy living here. The secluded cottage was the only residence in this area. He couldn't see a car and wondered if she had one. The door opened and Jim could see that Elinor had changed into a dress. She had been wearing jeans earlier and he had admired her shapely derriere. Now though, he could admire her shapely legs. He looked forward to getting to know her better and was intrigued by her aunt living in India.

Elinor had been worried that Jim wouldn't return so when she heard the knock at her door, she felt relieved, but also apprehensive that she may have invited a psychopath to dinner! Still, she couldn't live her life worrying about what might be and determined to enjoy herself, come what may.

The first thing Jim noticed as he entered the hall was that the cabinet seemed smaller, not quite as high as when he had carried it in and set it down. He mentally shook his head and thought his imagination was getting ahead of him. It was still locked though. Maybe there was a key in one of the many side drawers. He was drawn back to the present by the smell of dinner and his stomach growled in anticipation. He followed Elinor into the dining area, where the table was set for two.

"Am just about to serve up, Jim, hope you are hungry."

"I am starving! Here you are, a bottle of wine for you, I hope you like Rioja, just the soda water for me though. Do you need a hand with anything?"

"Just sit yourself down, if you open the wine and the soda water though, I will get the glasses. The corkscrew is in the drawer of the table if you need one." Elinor went off in the direction of the lounge and returned with two wine glasses, placing them on the table, and then to the kitchen where she filled two plates with the cottage pie. Placing the plates onto the place mats, she sat down and lifted her glass of red wine. "Cheers Jim, I hope you enjoy your soda water."

"So, tell me about yourself, how long have you

lived here?" enquired Jim. Elinor set her wine glass down.

"I was driving down the main road back last year when I noticed the turn-off. It was a beautiful day, the sea shone blue and sparkled in the sunlight so I came down the turn-off for a nose and found this cottage with a For Sale sign. I phoned the number on the sign and here I am! My husband died three years ago; he was driving too fast around a blind bend and hit a lorry that had broken down. He was killed instantly. The money from his life insurance, plus the sale of our flat meant I could not only afford the cottage but not worry about getting a job either. I sell antiques, but I buy online or go overseas for customers looking for specific items, so I don't need a shop and I have plenty of time to source the items. There are several pieces here that are antiques, this table is, plus the clock in the hall. That's what I was doing in Delhi, visiting my Aunt Gertrude and looking for something for a client. When I saw the cabinet I fell instantly in love with it, but I was due to fly home that afternoon so decided to leave it until my next visit. Gertrude saw an opportunity to gift it. Your turn now." Elinor started to eat.

Jim set his fork down. He had nearly finished eating, being so hungry he had practically wolfed it down. "Mmm, this is delicious. Well, where do I start? Firstly, I am divorced with no kids. My wife found someone else that she preferred to me. I work long hours with deliveries as I work for myself. The phone calls tell me what to pick up from the port and I collect the itinerary that tells me where to drop it off. The clients who ordered the goods pay me and I'm never out of work. I live in a small flat that I own not that far from here but with no sea view. My parents are elderly and I help them out whenever I can. They live fifty miles away so I don't get to see them as often as I would like. I love antiques; that cabinet of yours fascinates me. Have you tried to open it yet?" Jim resumed eating, clearing his plate.

Hmm, thought Elinor. Good looking, single, and cares about his parents, plus a love of antiques. Just my sort of guy. It must be my lucky day, a beautiful curiosity delivered by a handsome available man. Elinor couldn't help but smile.

"I was looking at it earlier, it glows in the sunlight. I did try opening it, with no luck. I haven't looked for a key though as I'm not one hundred percent sure that it needs one. This may sound daft, but I think that when the time is right, it will just open. There is such a mystical air about it." Now he will think I am dippy, thought Elinor.

Jim was drinking his soda water. He put his glass down and reached across the table to touch Elinor's hand.

"I don't think it's such a foolish perception, I handle a lot of strange goods in my line of work, quite a lot of antiques, and I must be honest, that cabinet makes the hair on the back of my neck stand on end. You are now going to think I'm daft, but I must say that when I picked it up at the quayside, I felt it tremor. I believe this Vihaan when he says that it always comes back! I would love to meet him and your aunt, plus visit the antiquity store. He must have some amazing stuff."

At that moment they both heard a click—the lid of the cabinet slowly rose open.

****

Getting up from the table they both nearly ran to the cabinet. Sure enough, the lid was rising. Elinor grabbed Jim's hand for support. The lid opened fully, offering up its contents for inspection. It was empty….and then the lid slowly closed and relocked itself.

"Well, that was strange!" exclaimed Jim. "Bit of an anti-climax don't you think?" Elinor wasn't so sure. Yes, the cabinet was empty, but perhaps it was hiding something else, for her eyes only?

"There must be a reason why it showed us that Jim. I need to give it some thought, maybe I need to speak to Vihaan, who knows more than he is giving away. My aunt is seeing him this week, at least, she is contacting him to let him know the cabinet arrived safely."

Jim checked the time on the clock above it. Giving Elinor's hand a quick squeeze, he let her go.

"Am going to make a move home now. Do you want to get your mobile and add my number? I'll take yours as well. We can talk tomorrow." Elinor went to get her phone and they exchanged numbers. Giving her a quick peck on her cheek, he thanked her for dinner and left.

Elinor was surprised he had left so early, but still, he did have work tomorrow. Meanwhile, she would have a nose through the drawers in the cabinet. But first, a coffee. She would finish the wine later. Heading for the kitchen she switched the kettle on and added coffee and milk to a mug. Whilst waiting for the kettle she mused on the events of the evening. She liked Jim; the more she saw of him, the keener she was on him. He seemed a caring person as well. She was ready for a relationship now, was he the one? The kettle boiled, Elinor added the water to her mug, stirred it, and took it to the dining table. Setting it down on a coaster, she walked over to the cabinet and slowly stroked the lid, feeling all the engravings set into the wood. She traced the one swirl that felt different from the others. The cabinet tremored and shook. Elinor retracted her hand, heard the lock click and the lid rose.

Out of the space between the lid and the cabinet, a mist started to swirl up, whirling and spinning above the cabinet forming a shape. A head started to form, and a voice spoke softly,

"Elinor, I am your servant, and your wish is my command." The cabinet continued to tremor.

"What….what are you?" stuttered Elinor.

"I am the genie of the cabinet, your wish is my command," the voice continued.

"But….but you didn't show earlier when the lid opened?" Elinor was feeling scared and out of her depth. What was going on here?

"I show myself only to you, my dear, not to

anyone else. Your wish is my command," the genie insisted in a seductive voice.

"But I don't command you to do anything, I don't need you, um, you can go now!" Elinor was shaking with fright.

"Elinor, Elinor don't be afraid of me, I have been waiting a long time for you. Your wish is my command." Elinor was wondering how to shut it down. It wasn't as if it was a laptop, just close the lid, and there you go, job done! Perhaps if she closed the lid of the cabinet? The genie must have been reading her mind.

"It doesn't work like that my dear, you summoned me remember."

Elinor wished that Jim was here, holding her hand. She walked back to the dining table and returned with her coffee. Perhaps a shot of caffeine would help her to think, what to do, what to say.

"Can I command you to return to Vihaan?" she asked hopefully.

"No, Elinor, you cannot. I don't belong to him, I belong to you. I have been waiting for you. Your wish—"

"Okay," interrupted Elinor. "I get it." Sipping her coffee, she had a sudden thought. "Can you make Jim fall in love with me?"

The genie sighed. "No Elinor, he isn't meant for you, he is promised to another."

Elinor was pretty sure that the genie wasn't what it said it was. After all, her wish was, etc., etc. The genie whirled and swirled and dropped level with Elinor's face. It revealed two bright blue eyes and a pink rosebud mouth that spread wide into a grin.

"I am what I say I am. Make a wish, there must be something that you want."

Elinor thought hard and then remembered something. "I only have three wishes, is that correct?" The genie grinned even wider.

"No, that is only in films and books. You can have as many wishes as you want, whenever you want. All you have to do is summon me. Now that I am out of the box, so to speak, I will be forever here. All you have to do is to call me by my name and I will appear." Elinor took another drink of her coffee.

"And what is your name?" she asked, wondering if this was her get out of jail free card.

"It is Genie of course, did I not tell you that? I am the genie of the cabinet and—oh, okay, you know the rest. I can see by the look on your face that you are not sure of me. I cannot do you any harm, my dear. Jim does like you, you don't have to make a wish for him to love you, but fate does have a plan for him, and that does not include you." Genie swirled and twisted above the cabinet and wondered if Elinor would believe her lies.

Taking her coffee mug back to the kitchen, she put it in the sink. The dishes from dinner were still waiting to be washed and her dishwasher wasn't working. Ah—she called out, "Genie, can you fix my dishwasher, please? That is, I wish for you to fix it—please."

A voice wafted from the hall. "Your wish is my command." The lights on the dishwasher came on.

Elinor opened the door, filled it up with the plates, cutlery, mugs, the casserole dish, the saucepan, added a dishwater tablet, and shut the door, choosing the wash she wanted. The dishwasher surged into action. Hmm, she thought, Genie could be useful after all. Walking back to the dining table she refilled her wine glass with the Rioja and sat down. Maybe she could live with the cabinet and her unexpected guest after all!

****

Elinor woke up the following morning to another bright and sunny day. Deciding that she would shower later, she dressed in jeans, T-shirt, and sneakers and went downstairs to the kitchen. Filling the kettle, she switched it on. Opening the dishwasher she removed a clean and sparkling mug. As she closed the door, she realised that the machine wasn't plugged in. It had cleaned all the dishes in a full wash cycle using no electricity, just water. Could the washing machine do the same? Elinor made her coffee and wandered over to the cabinet, which was now closed, and tapped on the lid.

"Genie?" she called quietly. No response. Tracing her fingers over the lid she found the swirl indent and pressed it. Nothing. Turning to the opposite wall, she removed the door key from a hook and unlocked the front door. Walking back for her mug, she returned to the door and noting that the cabinet was still closed, opened the front door and stepped outside.

Following the path around to the back of the cottage, Elinor made her way to the wooden steps that led to the beach. Sitting down on the top step, she slowly sipped her hot coffee and ruminated. Were the events of the previous evening, a dream? But, it couldn't have been, the dishwasher had definitely washed the dishes. Well, so much for the genie being out of the box, was she to be believed? Genie didn't come when Elinor called her. She looked over at the beach, it was her private beach that came with the cottage. The sand shone golden brown with the sea on its way in; the waves gently undulating along the shoreline. With the sun shining on the water, the sea shimmered, reflecting the blue sky. In the distance, there were a few seagulls, circling and calling out to each other. Elinor sighed with contentment. There wasn't much she could wish for, with her beautiful home, this view, and her own beach. Jim was not a figment of her imagination and she was looking forward to getting to know him better. She would ring her aunt later in the week and arrange another visit, and maybe Jim would accompany her this time. Drinking up her coffee, she set her empty mug down on the step and removed her sneakers. Getting up she grabbed the handrail and walked down the two flights of steps and stepped onto the sand, feeling the soft warm grains between her toes. Elinor closed her eyes soaking up the heat of the sun. The hand on her shoulder made her screech!

"Oh, sorry Elinor! I thought you might have

heard me coming down the steps. I saw that your front door was open, so guessed you wouldn't be far." She wheeled round and faced Jim.

"Thanks, I nearly had heart failure. Aren't you working today?" He set his arm around her shoulder and pulled her towards him.

"There were only two collections today, I've already delivered them and now I'm free for the rest of the day. Want to spend it with me?" Elinor leaned against him and again thought how lucky she was.

"That sounds like a plan. Let's go back to the cottage and I'll have a quick shower, unless you want me to meet you back here?" Jim looked down at her and agreed that it was too warm to be indoors, he would wait for her on the beach.

Elinor stood underneath the cool water of the shower, shampooing her short hair. Her pixie cut was easy to manage. At 5ft 4, she wasn't overly short, but compared to Jim—she barely came up to his shoulder. She would be 45 soon, she might suggest to him that they celebrate it in India, then she could introduce him to her Aunt Gertrude and Vihaan. Elinor needed no excuse to go back to Vihaan's store, another client was waiting for an antique. Giving another sigh of happiness, Elinor finished her shower, dried herself and her hair. Stepping back into her jeans, a fresh T-shirt, and sneakers, she made her way to the kitchen, then returned to the beach.

Whilst waiting for Elinor to return, Jim walked along the shoreline with his sandals in his hand. The water was cold and his toes were freezing. The warmth of the sand soon heated them back up though, as he made his way back to the steps. He sat on the bottom step with his legs stretched out, his feet drying in the sun. He had left his baseball cap on, guarding his bald head against the rays. Closing his eyes, he was nearly asleep when he heard Elinor making her way down the steps. Elinor handed him a mug.

"Coffee Sir, black with one sugar." Setting her drink down, she sat one step above him, being no room for two on the bottom step. Jim thanked her and they sat in a comfortable silence drinking their coffee.

"Did you know the beach came with the cottage when you first saw it?"

"Not at the time. Because of the high stone walls at the end of the road, I could only see the sea and part of the beach. I assumed the cottage just had the sea view. The owner told me when he met me with the keys - because of the design you can't see the steps from inside. It was only when I walked along the path at the side of the building that I saw the steps leading down to the beach. I was expecting a garden!"

Jim laughed. "That's where I expected to find you. Do you usually leave your front door open? I could have just gone in and waited for you, but that seemed rude." Elinor flipped his baseball cap off.

"And you still would have frightened me! Nobody ever comes down this road, except for deliveries. One sign at the top says, 'No through road' and the other, 'No Entry'. If anyone does drive down here at night, the security lights outside come on. So in all honesty, I feel safe leaving the door open unless I am intending to stay out here long. I was drinking my coffee on the top step, but the sand looked so inviting." Elinor stretched her legs out.

"I am getting stiff sat here, shall we walk along the beach?" Jim got up, retrieved his baseball cap, and offered his hand to Elinor which she took. He pulled her up off the step and still holding her hand they set off. The beach wasn't that big, more of a small cove that was sheltered from the wind.

"It must be awesome when the winds are up. How far does the sea come in?"

"Where it is now is nearly high tide. It doesn't go out that far either. I can sit on the steps quite safely when there is a storm, except of course it gets rather chilly." Elinor smiled up at him. Happiness radiated on her face.

"Right," said Jim, looking at his watch. "Can I take you for lunch? There is a lovely place not that far from here. I don't know about you, but this sea air gives me an appetite."

Elinor grabbed his wrist to look at his watch. "It's only 11.30, isn't that a bit early?"

"I was at the port for 6 am, that's why I didn't stay long last night. I am now ravenous. Besides, by the time we get there, it will be about 12. That is lunchtime!"

By noon they were sat outside a charming bistro waiting for their order of plaice and chips.

"So, did anything happen after I left last night? Did the cabinet reveal its secrets?" Jim teased Elinor, who blanched. Dare she tell him? He would think that she had lost the plot! He saw the look that passed across her features.

"You can tell me. I wouldn't be at all surprised if that cabinet had developed wings and flown around your cottage, or opened to reveal a magic carpet that swooped you up and took you across the English Channel." Jim reached out and took her hands in his.

"You aren't that far off the mark," Elinor still debating whether to tell him. Jim looked incredulous.

"Seriously?"

"Look, being honest with you Jim, if I do tell you, you're going to think I'm a nut job." At that point, their food arrived and Elinor breathed a sigh of relief.

Back at the cottage, the cabinet lid was open and Genie was swirling and twisting above it. She hadn't appeared when Elinor had called her because she knew that Jim was due, and she wouldn't show herself to him. She had nosed around the cottage in Elinor's absence when she was sure the two of them had left. She had heard Jim's car heading up the road so knew the coast was clear for her to appear. She also knew that Elinor was about to tell.

"Elinor," she breathed. "Don't tell him." But the genie knew that Elinor couldn't hear her.

As they ate their meal, Elinor had a feeling that she shouldn't tell Jim, but it was too late now. She had said too much already.

****

After they had eaten and were drinking coffee, Jim said, "Right Miss nut job, there was something I remembered whilst we were eating, about your cabinet. When I have the itinerary for the items I'm picking up, there are usually photos attached so that I know I have the right ones. Whilst I was waiting this morning for my pieces to clear customs, I got chatting to one of the other drivers. You are not going to believe this! I was telling him about your cabinet and Vihaan saying that it always returns to his antiquity store. Well, back last year this driver picked up the same cabinet. He recognised it from the itinerary sheet that was still in the van from yesterday. He delivered it to his client in London. A couple of days later, the client rang him to say that overnight the cabinet mysteriously disappeared. So Vihaan was telling you the truth. The cabinet is still in your cottage?"

Elinor was flabbergasted. "You only just remembered? And yes, it was still there when we left."

Jim looked apologetic. "With frightening you this morning it went out of my mind. The driver said that the client was hopping mad, but there wasn't anything he could do about it. So believe me when I say that anything you tell me won't surprise me!" Elinor leaned back in her chair and mulled over what to tell him. Decision made, she told him about the events after he had left.

"A genie? Really? Are you telling me that the cabinet is housing a real genie? That makes wishes come true? Oh My God. You have got to be kidding me, Elinor!" He laughed so hard he nearly fell off his chair. Elinor was sure he didn't believe her.

"Honest Jim, how could I possibly make it up? Anyway, she won't show herself to you so I have no way of proving it either, you're just going to have to accept what I told you." Between chuckles, Jim managed to spit out that he did believe her, it just wasn't what he was expecting to hear.

"So what should I do? I know you find it funny, but I don't think she tells the truth. The cabinet has clearly made itself at home and isn't going to disappear any time soon. I don't want a genie popping up anytime she feels like whispering....Your wish is my command, make a wish, you know you want to." Jim could see that Elinor wasn't happy, but he couldn't shift the cabinet, it was stuck hard to the floor.

"Why don't you ask Vihaan if he will accept it back? If you tell the genie that she isn't wanted, maybe she will let the cabinet be moved," suggested Jim.

Elinor thought hard. "I don't think the genie controls the cabinet. I think the cabinet has a mind of its own, it's just a house for the genie if that makes sense. I like the cabinet, but even that is mysterious just on its own."

Jim consulted his watch; they were already on their second coffee and it was now nearly 1.30 pm.

Times flies when something is interesting to talk about he reflected.

"What do you want to do next Elinor? We have the rest of the afternoon at our disposal. Do you want to go antique hunting or move on somewhere else that's quieter?" The bistro was starting to get busy.

"I will use the facilities here first, then let's go for a walk. I will treat us to an ice cream."

The cabinet lid was closed, Genie was sitting on the lid. She knew what Elinor had said, couldn't believe how astute Elinor was, plus she was getting far too close to Jim. Elinor belonged to her now. Jim was getting in the way. Hadn't she told her that he wasn't meant for her? Genie flew up in a rage. She would have to be far more ingenuous. Elinor had to give him up!

As they strolled along the seafront hand in hand enjoying their ice creams, Jim thought how lucky he was to have found Elinor. If it hadn't been for the cabinet, they wouldn't have met. He felt sure that it was meant to be. Finishing his ice cream, he turned towards Elinor and held her against his broad chest, resting his chin upon her head. She breathed him in. Lifting his head, he raised her chin and kissed her, a long lingering kiss. Elinor felt butterflies in her stomach, and her heart swelled with happiness. She blissfully kissed him back. She didn't need a genie, she had everything she could wish for. Jim dropped Elinor off back at the cottage later that afternoon. His mobile had rung a few times which meant he had a busy day tomorrow. With a promise that he would see her tomorrow night and take her out to dinner, he kissed her and drove off.

She opened her front door with a huge smile spread across her face, on cloud nine. Jim had kissed her! She practically floated through the door and was surprised to see that Genie was sat on the cabinet lid. Now in her full form, the genie sat with her legs crossed and barefooted. She was dressed in pale blue silk harem trousers that were cuffed at the ankle, plus a matching camisole top with spaghetti straps. Her clothes fitted her like a second skin. Her long blonde hair was twisted and tied with a matching blue silk ribbon, which hung over her left shoulder. She scowled at Elinor. Tempted as she was to ignore her, Elinor smiled sweetly at Genie and asked her if she was locked out.

"No Elinor, I was waiting for you, wanting to warn you again about Jim. You must leave him and never see him again, he will hurt you. He is meant for another," Genie insisted.

"We have free will, sweetie. You are my servant if I remember your words correctly? My wish is your command, and my wish is that you return to the cabinet and stay there until you are summoned!"

Elinor stalked off to the kitchen feeling pleased with herself. She was not going to let an ethereal being tell her what not to do. The genie swirled up and spun round and round. She was angry and was not going to be locked away. She had spent an eternity in that cabinet, waiting—.

Elinor made herself a coffee and took it to the lounge. Walking past the cabinet she noticed that there was no sign of Genie and breathed a sigh of relief. She needed to work out how to get rid of her, for good. As for the cabinet—sitting down and setting the mug on a coffee table, she picked up the remote and turned the television on. There was a wildlife documentary about to start that she wanted to watch. Although the programme was interesting, Elinor was distracted. She worried for Jim and the genie scared her. She would ask Jim if he had an axe, that cabinet needed to be destroyed, the sooner the better. Hopefully, without a home, the genie would leave.

Jim phoned Elinor the following day to say he would arrive at eight pm. Elinor asked him about an axe. He was surprised at her request but reasoned that she would explain when he saw her later. Driving down her road that evening, with a bouquet of roses on the passenger seat and an axe in the boot of his car, as he tried to slow down nearer the cottage, he found that his brakes weren't working. Instead, his car gathered speed. He was approaching the stone wall at the end of the road with no means of stopping the car. Realising that if he didn't do something, he was going to get seriously hurt, he opened his door and dove out onto the tarmac. The car smashed into the stone wall with an almighty crash. Elinor heard the sound of metal on stone and the crushing sound of steel. She flung open the front door and ran down the road in a panic. Jim was lying on the road, moaning. She ran to him and was relieved to see that he was okay, just bruised and shocked. She cradled him in her arms. As she looked at the car, she realised that it was a complete write-off. The bonnet was smashed: red rose petals floated in the air. Jim had had a lucky escape, if he hadn't thrown himself out of the car, he would have been killed.

Genie flung herself around the inside of the cabinet. Dammit, Jim wasn't dead! She worried about what Elinor might do next. If her home was destroyed—.

Elinor helped Jim into her home and sat him on the sofa. He was still looking white. Elinor left him to make him a strong drink with plenty of sugar. As she walked past the cabinet she could see that it was shaking. The sooner that thing was destroyed, the better she would sleep. Returning with a strong coffee made with three sugars, she sat down beside him. He gave her a weak smile.

"Can you wish my car back to health?" he asked wryly.

"If we can still open the boot of your car, I want that bloody axe!"

"I was going to ask you about that. Is it for, *the, um, you know what*?" asked Jim quietly, now regaining his strength. He realised that something must have happened if Elinor was wanting it destroyed. She told him that the genie had been waiting for her yesterday.

"She is adamant that you are not meant for me, and said that I should leave you and never see you again. I think she only wants me for herself, and look what happened with your car? In fact, what did happen Jim?" Elinor was talking in a very low voice.

"My brakes failed, the car was only serviced last week. My brakes were fine until I tried to slow down before your cottage. The brakes wouldn't work and the car speeded up instead. I didn't have time to use the handbrake, I just opened my door and flung myself out. You don't think it was an accident, do you?" Jim sat up and hugged Elinor to him.

"No, I don't Jim, I'm terrified. She isn't going to hurt me, at least, I don't think she will, but you are definitely in danger. Is that what happened to my husband? Genie keeps saying that she has been waiting for me. So, yes, I am going to do something about it! Meanwhile what about food? Shall I order in?" Jim looked at Elinor.

"That sounds like a good idea, but why don't you make us both another cuppa first? There is something I need to do for you."

Elinor looked at him, puzzled. Placing his lips close to her ear, he murmured, "You aren't going to lose me to a genie. Leave the bitch to me, my darling." Moving his mouth to hers, he kissed her.

Elinor got up and turning to him, whispered, "Be careful," and blew him a kiss. Picking up his empty mug, she went to the kitchen and heard him quietly open the door. Elinor smiled to herself. Filling the kettle and switching it on, she put his mug in the sink and got two clean ones. Whilst waiting for him to return, she pondered. He was such a caring man, he knew without asking what needed to be done. As the kettle started to boil, she heard the door open, and Jim called out to her.

"Coffee nearly ready? I won't be long."

Elinor waited for the sound of the axe. Nothing. Elinor made the drinks. Still nothing from the hall. She stirred them both, listening, but not hearing anything. Curious now as to what Jim was doing, Elinor picked up the mugs and made her way back to the lounge. As she approached the hall though, there was no sign of him. The cabinet lid was closing with a mist creeping back inside.

There was no sign of Jim, nor the axe.

****

Elinor was distraught. Setting down the mugs on the dining table, she ran to the cabinet. A last tendril of mist slipped into the cabinet as the lid closed and locked. Elinor hammered her fists on it and called out to Jim, demanded the genie to open up and let him go. There was only an ominous silence from within. Feeling sick with worry, she turned towards the dining table. Grabbing her mobile and coffee, she headed out of the door towards the safety of the steps heading down to the beach and sat on the top step holding her phone in one hand and her coffee in the other. She needed to phone her aunt and ask her to get hold of Vihaan but then realised that it was past one in the morning in Delhi. What was she to do? Looking out at the calm sea, she sipped her coffee. She couldn't phone the police, but if someone drove down her road they would see Jim's car and report it. With Jim gone—gone where though? Thoughts raced through her mind. Would the cabinet return to Vihaan's store? Was Jim dead? Would she be suspected of murdering him? She realised that the only safe option she had was to head for the airport and get the first flight out to Delhi. Maybe Vihaan would know what to do, or who to contact if he didn't. Elinor couldn't risk the genie knowing her intentions.

Getting up off the step, Elinor turned back towards the cottage. Pushing open her front door, she went silently through the cottage, packing a backpack with essentials plus her passport, visa, and Indian Rupees that she had from previous trips. Her visa, fortunately, was still valid. Checking her purse for her bank and credit cards, she shoved that into her backpack along with her mobile. She stopped only long enough to rinse out the coffee mugs, dry them, and put them back in the kitchen cupboard. With her car keys and backpack in one hand, she removed the door key from the hook in the hall and let herself out. Locking the front door she headed to the garage where her car was parked

Elinor arrived in Delhi the following afternoon. She phoned her aunt from the airport to tell her that she was getting a taxi and would be with her shortly.

"Gertrude, can you ask Vihaan to come over? I need to talk to both of you. Something terrible has happened and I haven't a clue what to do or who to turn to. I will explain when I get to your house."

Gertrude opened her front door as the taxi pulled up. Elinor climbed out and fell into her aunt's arms

33

sobbing. Gertrude led her inside and sat her down. There was a pot of chai brewing.

"Whatever has happened my darling?" asked Gertrude. "Vihaan is on his way, he won't be long. Should we wait for him before you explain?"

"Yes, Gertrude, am hoping he might have some answers," replied Elinor between shuddering sobs."

At that moment Vihaan arrived having found Gertrude's door open. He looked at Elinor and knelt by her side, taking her hand in his.

"Is this to do with the cabinet?" he asked her.

Gertrude poured tea for them all as Vihaan settled himself on the couch next to Elinor. She blew her nose and tried to calm herself.

"I had better start from the beginning," looking at Vihaan, and then Gertrude who was now sat opposite her. Leaning forward Elinor picked up her cup of tea and held it in both of her hands, drawing comfort from the fragrance.

"The cabinet was delivered by a lovely man, by the name of Jim. He brought it in and it settled itself in my hall. He couldn't pick it up later on when he tried, it was stuck fast to the floorboards. That's when I realised that it wasn't going to re appear in your store, Vihaan. I was looking for a key for the lock, but there wasn't one, so I surmised that maybe there wasn't a key, that the lid would open when the cabinet was ready." Elinor turned her head towards Vihaan who nodded. Elinor continued. "Sure enough, later that evening I heard the lock click and the lid opened. I had invited Jim to dinner so he was with me. When we looked though, the cabinet was empty and then it promptly closed. I wondered if it was because Jim was there. After he left, I was looking at the cabinet and tracing the intricate patterns on the lid. The sun had been shining on it and it seemed to glow. Then, I heard a click and the lid opened."

Vihaan and Gertrude looked at each other. Elinor wasn't sure that she understood the unspoken words that passed between them in that one glance. She finished her tea and set her cup down on the table. Neither of them said a word, but he nodded at her to continue.

"This is where it gets complicated and I'm not sure you are both going to believe me." Though Elinor had her suspicions that what she was going to say next was not going to be that much of a surprise to either of them.

"Carry on Elinor," said Vihaan. "I can assure you that where that cabinet is concerned, nothing would make me disbelieve you. I never told you this, but it usually hid in my store whenever it returned. The day you and Gertrude visited, I swear it moved so that you would see it."

It was Elinor's turn to look at Gertrude as she realised what Vihaan's glance had meant.

"A mist swirled up and out of the mist a disembodied voice spoke to me. 'Elinor, I am your servant and your wish is my command.' The voice continued. 'I am the genie of the cabinet, your wish is my command.' A head started to form, then bright blue eyes, followed by rosebud pink lips. I then asked why it hadn't shown itself before and it replied, 'I show myself only to you, my dear, not to anyone else. Your wish is my command.' By now I was frightened and it knew I was scared because then it said, 'Elinor, Elinor don't be afraid of me, I have been waiting a long time for you. Your wish is my command.' I was wondering how to get rid of it and again as if it was reading my thoughts, I got this reply, 'It doesn't work like that my dear, you summoned me.' And, and…" Elinor started to cry again.

Vihaan took her hand and sent another look to Gertrude, who nodded. She picked up the teapot and went off to the kitchen. Gertrude returned with a tray to collect the teacups, milk, and sugar. Moments later she was back with a bottle of wine and three wine glasses. Vihaan took the bottle from her, opened it, and then poured the wine into the glasses. Vihaan handed a wine glass to Gertrude who was still looking pale and then passed a glass to Elinor.

"What happened to Jim? I know djinns can be possessive."

Elinor took the glass with a weak smile. "Thank you Vihaan. Jim was going to destroy the cabinet with an axe. Genie, the name she gave for herself, kept saying that Jim was meant for another and to leave him. On his way to my house last night, his car crashed into the beach wall when his brakes failed. He had to jump out of the car while it was moving. When that failed to kill him, and he was about to destroy the cabinet, one minute he was there, and then he just vanished into thin air along with the axe. That's when I left and came here. I don't know what to do. I love him so much—is there a chance he could still be alive? Could he be standing in your store?"

Gertrude looked aghast, her face went white. "Oh, what have I done? It's all my fault for sending it to you!"

"Please don't blame yourself, Gertrude, I was the one who wanted the damn thing. I was going to arrange for it to be delivered the next time I came here to see you. How were you to know what secrets it was hiding?" Elinor looked at Vihaan. "I'm sure you didn't know either or else you would have destroyed it yourself or tried to. Jim was trying to protect me and now he has gone...." Elinor trailed off and the tears coursed down her cheeks.

"What happens to a djinn if its home is destroyed?" Gertrude asked Vihaan. He replied very quietly, "It dies. That's why Jim has disappeared. I have no idea where he could be, but on a positive note, if the djinn didn't want him for herself, he might turn up somewhere or someplace else. Am not really sure. I need to think who to ask, who might know."

The room went deathly silent.

****

Vihaan, Gertrude, and Elinor sipped their wine, each absorbed in their own thoughts. Elinor looked up and remarked that she had been intending to bring Jim to visit on her 45th birthday. He loved antiques and wanted to meet Gertrude and Vihaan.

"He didn't laugh at me when I revealed the cabinet's secret, well, yes, he did laugh, but only because it was the last thing he had expected to hear. Neither of you though seem that surprised?" Elinor rhetorically asked, not expecting an answer. It was Gertrude that replied.

"It's part of India's folklore, we all believe in djinns, even if we haven't seen one. I find it fascinating that there was one hiding in the cabinet. I know that she has done something to the person that you love, and I hope that he is somewhere safe, but I must admit that it was the last thing I expected to hear. Genies aren't always confined to brass lamps, however, who would have guessed that the cabinet was hiding one." Gertrude lapsed into silence. She was pretty sure that Vihaan had known or suspected, after all, cabinets don't just reappear and hide. She looked over at Vihaan, who had the grace to blush.

"I did have my suspicions, Gertrude," said Vihaan, as though he had read her thoughts. He had known her for so many years and being such close friends, he was in tune with her.

"But if I had voiced my theory, no one would have believed me."

"And I would still have purchased it from you, Vihaan. So please, neither of you should feel guilty. Just my luck to pick a jealous one." Elinor tried to laugh, but failed, miserably.

Vihaan checked his watch, put down his empty glass, and rose from the couch.

"I'm going to check my store. Now that you are here, we don't know if the cabinet is still in your cottage, or if Jim has inexplicably appeared. I'll be back shortly though, then I will take us all out for dinner. Save you cooking for us all, Gertrude." He leaned over and kissed her on the cheek.

"I will ring you if I see anything or anyone." Turning back to Elinor, he kissed her on the cheek as well.

"Try not to worry, you are safe here and we will try to find a solution." With that, he left the room.

Gertrude got up, moved across to Vihaan's vacant spot, and sat next to Elinor. She picked up Elinor's hand and held it in both of hers. "I love Vihaan, and if this had happened to him, I would be as distressed as you are. Strange things do happen you know. Jim might well appear somewhere unexpected, alive and well, but confused as hell. The only problem you will have then is getting him home without his passport." Elinor looked at Gertrude and burst out laughing, surprising both of them.

"That would take some explaining at the British Embassy, especially as there would be no evidence to show how he got here—by magic carpet perhaps?" Both of them dissolved into a fit of giggles. Elinor was relieved that Gertrude and Vihaan had believed her without question.

****

Back at Elinor's cottage, Genie was sat on the

39

cabinet mulling over the events of the previous evening. After her tantrum inside her home, she had become aware of movement in the hall. She had heard Elinor entering the kitchen and filling the kettle, then the front door opening. Curious as to what was going on, and worried as to what Jim might be up to, she had crept out of the cabinet and sat on the lid. She saw the front door open as Jim came back in and called out to Elinor.

"Coffee nearly ready? I won't be long." As he turned his head he had seen Genie in her full form sitting on the cabinet. His mouth had dropped open forming a soundless O. When Genie had spotted the axe in his hand, her eyes had blazed dark blue with fury. Before Jim had a chance to even raise the axe, the djinn had flown up in an incandescent rage, turning into a whirlwind of pure energy. She whirled and whipped, causing a vortex around him. The axe separated from his hand. It went spinning off in one direction and Jim in another. She neither knew nor cared where he had gone. Elinor belonged to her now. As Genie had swooped back into her home leaving a trail of mist in her wake, the lid had shut and locked itself. She only realised that Elinor had also left when she heard the front door being locked. Now she wondered where she was.

****

Vihaan was deep in thought as he walked back to his store after leaving Gertrude's house. He had always wondered about the strange cabinet. Every

40

time it returned to his store, it would hide, probably hoping Vihaan wouldn't find it too soon. One time he had spotted it on top of an antique wardrobe and had spluttered, "What the—how the heck did you get up there?" The following day it had gone, and after much searching, he had found it at the very back of his shop, behind a dresser. It just wasn't possible for a piece of furniture to return itself after being sold and installed in a new owners' home, let alone then play hide and seek!

When Elinor had entered his antiquity shop with Gertrude, it had blatantly made its approach to the front so that it was in full view. Vihaan just never knew where he was going to find it. He had lost count of the number of people who had purchased the damn thing, only to get a phone call within days to say that the item of furniture had upped and walked. He did try to talk a buyer out of the purchase, without much success.

And now this—he had told Gertrude about the cabinet's strange behaviour and she had laughed, saying that it just hadn't found a home it liked yet. If only he had known what the cabinet had been hiding all these years, and who it had been waiting for.

As he approached his shop, he removed his keys from his jacket pocket, inserted the shop key into the lock, and pushed the handle down. He opened the door and entered the dark interior. Feeling for the light switch and turning it on, the store lit up. Closing the door behind him, he walked towards his desk and sat down. Pulling open a drawer, Vihaan took out his Rolodex and placed it on his desk. He flicked through the cards looking for one in particular. Finding the one he wanted, he punched in the phone number on his desk phone, pressed the speaker button, and waited for the call to connect.

He was calling Delia, whom he had met last year at an antique fair. He had been at his wits' end at the time and had mentioned the strange piece of furniture that kept returning after it had been sold. Only that week yet another purchaser had rung to say that their item had vanished overnight. He had suggested that they contact their insurers as it had seemed to have been stolen, only to be told that the house alarm hadn't gone off and the police were scratching their heads. Vihaan could hardly tell them that the cabinet would probably return to him. Delia had heard about this, as it was a client of hers that had made the purchase. At the time she had thought that it had been stolen and didn't pay much attention, but now she was intrigued and had asked Vihaan if she could see it. A few days later she had visited him and they had both spent ages looking for it. They finally found it lurking in the darkest corner and were surprised to see that the lid was unlocked and open. Vihaan had never seen that happen before and had never found a key either. The cabinet was empty and within a couple of minutes, the lid had closed with a click. The two had looked at each other and Vihaan had said that it was the first time it had happened. Delia asked about the provenance, but all he knew was that it was there when his father had inherited the antiquity store, with no paperwork that he knew of and his father never talked about it. Delia had taken some photographs of it, intending to do some research, but Vihaan didn't hear from her again. Now he wondered if she had found out anything.

Delia answered his call and remembered him and his mysterious cabinet. He explained to her what had happened and the secret the cabinet had been hiding.

"So, Delia, I was wondering if you had done any research regarding the provenance and might have any idea what on earth I should do next. Do you know anything about djinns?" For a few moments, there was silence on the other end of the telephone and Vihaan waited for a response.

"Delia?"

"Vihaan, sorry, I can't believe what I am hearing! You are saying that your friend's niece has the cabinet and it's a home for a genie as well? And her boyfriend has disappeared?"

"Um, well, yes, I haven't looked around my store yet to see if either Jim or the cabinet is here, because, well, to be honest, I'm not expecting to find anything. I haven't a clue what to do or where to start looking. I mean, could he still be alive?"

Delia could hear the panic and distress in his voice.

"I can be with you within half an hour Vihaan. Meanwhile see if the cabinet has returned, which from what you have told me, I seriously doubt. I did find out something by the way. I will explain more when I see you. We will put our heads together and see what to do next."

The call disconnected and Vihaan put the Rolodex back in the drawer. With a heavy sigh, he got up. He would have a look around his store and see what he could find.

****

Delia arrived within half an hour. She was quite tall and slim, with eyes the colour of molasses and an olive tone to her skin. An attractive lady roughly the same age as Elinor, with dark shoulder-length hair. Vihaan hadn't seen anything or anyone. He had even called out Jim's name just in case, but there was only silence. There was no sign of the cabinet and he had looked in all the dark corners and shadows. Delia sat at Vihaan's desk, whilst he paced, unable to sit still. Delia had something to tell him.

"For goodness sake Vihaan, sit down."

He got another chair and joined her at his desk.

"Right, this is what I know. I asked my father first as he grew up here. He remembers this being an antiquity store when he was a child and also in my grandfather's youth. There were rumours then about an antique piece of furniture that reappeared whenever it was sold, but no one ever believed them. None of the shop owners would admit to the rumours being valid and eventually, people either forgot about them or thought that they were made up. I didn't tell you at the time because I wanted to find out more, but I haven't been able to find out much else. However, I did ring my father before I left to ask him if he knew anything about djinns. I think you already know that destroying a djinn's house, will kill the djinn if it doesn't get a chance to find a new home first. Now, seeing that an attempt has already been made to destroy the cabinet, we need to act quickly, before she realises that another attempt is likely to happen. Once the djinn is dead, the person who disappeared will in all likelihood return as the djinn will no longer be able to keep the person away."

Vihaan regarded Delia whilst he thought. "Is there another way to kill the djinn without destroying the cabinet? You see, Elinor loves the cabinet and it seems to have settled in her cottage. Without the presence of the genie, the cabinet will more than likely stay put, and Elinor can have her life back with Jim. There is a danger to Elinor I think if the genie realises her intentions. There must be another solution."

He drummed his fingers on the desk. He was worried that Elinor would end up disappearing as well, and anyone else that attempted to destroy the cabinet. As he was thinking, he suddenly remembered old lore.

"Isn't a silver knife coated in lamb's blood supposed to kill a djinn? I'm sure I recall old lore regarding djinns."

He suddenly felt a great weight being lifted. He was sure that was the answer. Delia agreed that this could be a better solution, except, "We still have the problem though that the genie won't trust Elinor, and who will do the killing? You said the genie only shows to Elinor, there is no way she could use a knife without the genie seeing it, surely?"

Vihaan decided that Delia should meet Gertrude and Elinor. He phoned the restaurant and reserved a table, and then phoned Gertrude. They would meet up at the restaurant and they could then discuss it and see if they could come up with a better plan. Delia was pleased to be invited and meet up with Vihaan's friends.

****

After Vihaan had made the introductions, the group sat down and ordered their food and drinks. The wine arrived and Delia told them what she knew about the age of the cabinet, and how a client of hers had purchased it the previous year.

"It was delivered to him in London, and he was pleased that it had arrived by sea within a matter of weeks. Then, two days later, my customer phoned me. I think you all might guess as to why. When Vihaan told me about an item of furniture that he was having problems with, I asked him if I could see it. I hadn't believed my client when he said that his purchase had disappeared overnight, I thought it must have been stolen." Delia laughed. "However, there can't be that many antiques that return themselves."

Elinor gasped. "That is what Jim told me a few days ago. He had been talking to the driver that delivered it. The customer had phoned him to complain, though as the driver told Jim, he had only delivered it. What happened after that wasn't his problem. He recognised the photo that was on the itinerary that Jim had, after delivering the cabinet to me. This is so weird, but at least, Delia, you know now that it is the truth, strange as it is."

"Not as strange as to how long it took Vihaan and myself to find it in his store. It was well hidden, and the lid was open!" Delia looked at Vihaan and he nodded.

"It was empty and within a couple of minutes, the lid closed and locked itself. I should have realised then that there was something else going on with that cabinet," he replied. Gertrude and Elinor were shocked at this revelation.

"You never told me that, Vihaan," said Gertrude.

"Well, it hadn't occurred to me at that point that something might be hiding in it, Gertrude," Vihaan replied. "It's only now that the genie has revealed itself. What I don't understand is, why was it waiting for Elinor?"

"I used to take Elinor into your store when she was a child, maybe that is when the cabinet fixated on her perhaps? I never used to see what that child was doing when I was talking to you and your father." Gertrude turned towards Elinor, who was sat on her right.

"Do you remember playing with the cabinet?"

"Well, I don't remember chasing it around the store, Gertrude," laughed Elinor. "But seriously, I don't recollect seeing it. I think you only took me a few times?"

"But, that cabinet does enjoy a game of hide and seek, Elinor. Think on it," suggested Vihaan.

At that point, their food arrived and after they had eaten, Vihaan ordered more wine.

"Right, now we need to think about how to separate the djinn from the cabinet. Am I right in thinking that you want to keep it, Elinor, if we can get rid of that genie for you?" asked Vihaan.

"I do love that antique, and from what Delia has said, am not surprised that it has settled in my sixteenth century cottage. It is a very old piece of furniture and it has made itself at home there. Did you tell Delia how it glows in the sunlight? As soon as Jim set it down in my hallway, under the antique clock, it quite literally set its clawed feet into the hardwood floor. I said to Jim that I'm sure that the genie and the cabinet are two separate entities. That cabinet is mysterious just as it is." Elinor teared up as she thought of Jim. "Do you think that Jim might return once we have got rid of its occupant?" she asked, hopefully.

"Well, that's the theory, Elinor. Now, I do seem to remember old lore regarding a silver knife coated in lamb's blood." Vihaan's voice went quiet. "But, how to use it on the genie is another matter. I don't want you or anyone else to suddenly disappear."

At that point Delia's mobile rung. Apologising to the others, Delia answered it when she realised that it was her father ringing her. Delia set her phone down on the table and put it on speaker so that they could all hear him. What he had to say surprised all of them.

"Delia," his voice resonated through the phone. "I made some calls after you rang me earlier, and I think I may have a solution to your friend's problem." The rest of the group listened with hope in their hearts. He continued, "You know your uncle Rupert is a bit eccentric, well, anyway, I recalled his passion for djinns after we spoke. He says that you need an old brass oil lamp. Rupert knows Vihaan by the way. He asked if he still has that enigmatic vanishing cabinet and if so, can he buy it?" Delia gave a sigh.

"Can you get to the point, dad?" They could hear him chuckling down the phone. "Yeah, yeah. Right. You need an old brass oil lamp, whatever you do, don't rub it!" Another laugh rumbled. "Get some iron filings and pour some into the lamp. Now, this is the tricky part. You need to either get the djinn into the lamp or, pour the contents of the lamp into the thingy that the djinn is residing in. Whichever way, iron is poison to a djinn. It will wail a lot and then disappear into a puff of smoke. Night Delia, let me know how it works out." The phone went silent.

Elinor burst into tears, tears of relief. "Oh, do you think that could work?" she sobbed, not asking anyone in particular. Delia put her hand on Elinor's.

"Yes, I do believe it would. All we need of course is a lamp, why brass though, I wonder?"

Vihaan answered, "Because that's where genies usually hide. As the one in the cabinet is probably happy where she is, I doubt that we will be able to persuade her to move, so, we will need to pour the filings into the cabinet, and that will be, as your

49

father put it, Delia, tricky."

Gertrude contributed with, "And we need a brass lamp, anyone? Vihaan?" Gertrude had her doubts that this would work but kept her thoughts to herself. Gertrude turned her head to speak to Elinor, her eyes widened, and she prodded her.

"Look, look on the windowsill. Can you see it?" Elinor turned to where Gertrude was pointing and sure enough, she saw it too. Delia looked as well, curious as to what had caught their attention, then said to Vihaan, "Do you know the owner of this restaurant? Because look what's on the windowsill."

Vihaan saw what they had noticed and he gave them all a big grin.

"Yes, I know the owner and am sure he would let us borrow it." With that, he got up out of his chair and headed towards the reception part of the restaurant and asked to speak to Arjun, and told them where he was sitting. He got back to the table and sat down. He was about to ask Delia about her uncle when he felt a tap on his shoulder. He turned in his seat and saw Arjun beaming at him. Vihaan got up and the two men hugged.

"Vihaan, it's good to see you." He greeted Gertrude and Elinor and shook hands with Delia.

"I trust you enjoyed your meal." He looked at Vihaan. "You should have let me know you were coming tonight." Vihaan beamed and said that it was a last-minute decision. "I asked to see you Arjun because I have a favour to ask, a strange request really, but I will try to explain as briefly as possible. You see, we need to capture a djinn and a reliable source has said that a brass lamp would do the job, just like that one on your windowsill. Could I borrow it?"

"Oh, you are pulling my leg, aren't you? I mean, sure you can borrow it, have it, it's only used as a decoration. But, are you serious? I mean, a djinn? Like a genie?" Arjun laughed uneasily. "Djinns are scary."

"Sadly, Arjun, I am serious."

"Sit back down, I will grab another chair and join you." Arjun had blanched. He got a chair from the next table and positioned it by Vihaan. He called one of the waiters over, ordered more drinks, and told him that Vihaan and his party were his guests, and to not bill Vihaan for the drinks and food. Arjun asked Vihaan to continue.

"Gertrude's niece, you remember Elinor of course, has that cabinet, you know the one I mean. It was hiding a secret, Arjun. It settled itself in Elinor's cottage and the lid opened. There was a djinn hiding in there," he paused.

Arjun looked even paler. The waiter arrived with another bottle of wine and five balloon glasses of brandy.

Vihaan continued, "The djinn was jealous of Elinor's boyfriend, and now he has disappeared, literally, into thin air. We haven't a clue whether he is dead or alive."

"Djinns can be very mean and spiteful, I know from experience," said Arjun, who picked up his brandy glass and swallowed the contents.

Gertrude looked at Arjun with consternation.

"What happened?" she asked, voicing what the others were thinking.

"You don't want to know. Suffice to say it did not end well. But, if you know of a way to get rid of it, and it works, please let me know."

Vihaan murmured to Arjun, "I think we need to talk. Can I pop by tomorrow morning, about 10 am?" Arjun patted Vihaan on his shoulder and pushed his chair back. Getting up, he walked over to the windowsill and picked up the brass lamp. Putting it on the table, he said, "Good luck my friend, I will see you in the morning." Saying goodbye to the rest of the group, he walked towards his office.

Gertrude, Elinor, and Delia were looking worried.

"That sounded rather ominous, do you think he will tell you tomorrow? He looked awful grim," asked Elinor.

"Arjun and I have been friends for a long time. He trusts me and knows that anything he tells me will be in confidence. But, you are right Elinor. If he wasn't willing to tell us now, then he could well have second thoughts."

Delia picked up the brass lamp and turned it in her hands. She murmured,

"Beautiful, it truly is, beautiful. The only way to get anything into it though is through the top. We will need a funnel, as well as iron filings." She put the lamp back on the table. No one else dared to pick it up.

"Is there a hardware shop in Deli?" asked Elinor. "Otherwise I can buy what we need online and get it delivered to my home."

Vihaan thought about it and said, "That might be a better idea, Elinor. You will need to return home soon anyway before your genie gets concerned as to where you are and what you are doing. I think it might be a good idea for one of us to return with you, you will need a distraction in place for this plan to work." Vihaan looked at Delia. "The djinn won't know you, Delia, are you able to go with Elinor? You can give the impression that you are on holiday."

Elinor laughed and said, "My cottage has its own

private beach, Delia. We will be able to fill the lamp without being seen by the djinn, we will just have to watch what we say, as I'm sure she listens. You never know, she might even show herself to you. As you are female, she shouldn't see you as a threat."

Delia grinned in delight. "I think that is a great idea, I could do with a break. Plus, I will have an excuse to have another look at that cabinet."

Vihaan lifted his brandy glass and proposed a toast. "To the despatching of djinns!" he said with a smile.

Delia and Elinor decided to leave Delhi the next day, catching a lunchtime flight. It was a nine and a quarter-hour flight, plus the drive back to the cottage. They would get to Elinor's around 11 pm.

The rest of the group finished their brandies, and got ready to leave, with Delia returning home to pack a bag and get some sleep.

"If you order the filings this evening, Elinor, we should have everything we need by the weekend. I have a funnel at home, I will bring it with me unless you already have one?"

Elinor replied, "I can't remember if I have a funnel," wrinkling her nose whilst she thought. "Bring yours please, Delia. One less thing to worry about. Will you take the brass lamp with you as well? That needs to be well hidden from the genie. I don't want to risk her seeing it before we are ready. Thank you for doing this. It's a big ask of someone that doesn't know me." Elinor hugged Delia.

The next day, Elinor and Delia were buckling themselves into their seats, ready for take-off. They had been lucky in purchasing the last remaining seats on the flight from Delhi and were due to land at Heathrow at ten-fifteen pm. Having only their hand luggage, they would only need to go through passport control.

"Poor Arjun, I wonder if Vihaan knows what happened to him, he hadn't returned before I left."

Delia thought, then said slowly, "Anything you ask of a djinn comes at a price. People think that they just grant wishes, but nothing is granted without a payment in other ways. Arjun, unfortunately, has found that out."

"But, the genie got my dishwasher working, although, I must admit, she didn't fix it, as I realised afterwards because it wasn't plugged in."

"She used her magic to impress you. She will be waiting now for you to ask her to grant a wish. Don't mention Jim, or wish for him to return, as you won't know the price she will extract from you until after the wish has been granted."

Elinor realised that Delia's knowledge of djinns must have been gleaned from her uncle.

"How much does your uncle know about them?"

"Enough to know that they are spiteful and ruthless. They don't care what pain they inflict and will do anything to prevent their home from being destroyed. We will have to be very canny in our dealings with your one, especially as she has attached herself to you." Delia looked at Elinor. "I asked my uncle last night about the best way to get her into the lamp, he suggested inviting her to take a look inside, before we have added any iron. If we can get her to do that, by bunging the spout so she can't get back out, we could then take her far away from the cabinet."

"And then what? Could we still add the iron filings through the top without her escaping?" Elinor felt a frisson of excitement. "Or just toss the lamp into the harbour with her trapped inside. And what do we bung the spout with?" Elinor realised that she was bombarding Delia with questions.

Delia laughed. "One question at a time, Elinor! OK, I found a small rubber stopper in my kitchen drawer which is a perfect fit for the spout, along with a small silver funnel. If we dip the stopper and the stem of the funnel into some glue and then into the iron filings, as soon as we lift the top of the lamp and insert the funnel, the iron on the stem will prevent her from escaping through the funnel. All we have to do then is pour some filings into the lamp, remove the funnel and replace the top of the lamp. Then we can do what we like with the lamp!"

Elinor sat back in her seat. Whilst they were chatting the plane had taken off and was ascending into the clouds. Her ears started to pop and she hurriedly put a mint into her mouth and offered one to Delia, who gratefully accepted. There was silence between them as they sucked hard on the sweet.

Elinor gave a big sigh. "What if the djinn won't enter the lamp? I don't suppose your uncle had that answer?" Delia touched Elinor's hand.

"Let's take it one step at a time. If we can't entice her in, then, we will just have to work out how to tip the filings into the cabinet."

"Shame we can't drill a hole in the top of it. That would make it easier," Elinor replied ruefully.

Delia looked at Elinor in shock, "Oh no, that would upset the cabinet! Christ knows what that would make it do."

"I hadn't thought of that. But, you are right. The cabinet is another entity entirely. I hope it will be happy when we get rid of its occupier, otherwise, we could be opening another can of worms. Oh, Delia, what have I got myself into? I wish I had never set eyes on it now."

"I think your aunt had a point when she said that you used to play in the antiquity store when you were a child. The cabinet must have spotted you, otherwise, why else did it make the effort to get to the front of the store when you arrived? Even Vihaan said he was surprised as it usually lurked in the darkest corner it could find. Are you sure you don't remember?"

"I must admit, I haven't given it much thought, since Gertrude mentioned it. I must have been about ten years old at the time. Maybe it did play a game of hide and seek with me. I will have to try and remember, but it can wait until this problem is solved. I'm scared to sleep in my cottage now, on my own. Thank goodness you are staying with me for a while."

Elinor undid her seat belt and turned towards Delia. "Promise me you will be careful. I couldn't deal with you doing a vanishing act as well."

"Don't worry, I have no intention of upsetting your genie, in fact, the opposite. You wait and see.

Now, let's get some rest, read a book, and stop worrying. We can't do anything whilst we are stuck on a plane."

Delia undid her seat belt, leaned forward, and retrieved a paperback from her backpack. Elinor did the same and they both sat quietly reading.

****

It was just on eleven-thirty that evening when Elinor stopped in front of her garage. Pressing the remote on her key fob, the garage door rose and Elinor drove in and stopped the car. They both got out and stretched, tired and stiff from the journey back to the cottage. Taking the backpacks out of the car, they both left the garage, and Elinor locked it. She showed Delia the path that led to the steps for the beach. The outside security lights had come on automatically as they had walked towards the cottage, the path could be seen.

"Come on in," said Elinor, as she unlocked the front door and switched on the lights. The cabinet was still in the hall, its clawed feet set into the hardwood floor. It wasn't intending on moving anytime soon. Delia gasped when she saw it.

"Oh my, it is beautiful. Just look at all the carvings. No wonder you wanted it." Her gaze wandered towards the legs and feet of the cabinet.

"Those look like real claws, Elinor. Crikey, it really has set itself into your floor and made itself at home." She stroked the top of the lid, which felt warm to the touch. The rosewood seemed to gleam under the spotlights in the hall. Delia felt as though she was touching something alive, rather than an inert object. Lifting her hand she turned towards Elinor and gave her a mischievous grin.

"Come on, let's have a drink, Delia. You must be parched, I know I am. Do you want a hot drink or a glass of wine? We need to unwind." They went into the lounge where Delia sank on the sofa with a sigh.

"A glass of wine sounds good. Have you got any white?" she asked Elinor, who nodded with a smile, removed two wine glasses from an antique dresser, and placed them on the coffee table. Turning towards the hall, Elinor went to the kitchen to get a bottle from the fridge. Passing the cabinet, she ran her hand over the top as she walked past it. The wood felt warm under her fingertips. It was hard to believe what was contained within.

Returning with a bottle of Chardonnay, Elinor walked past the cabinet with bated breath, anxious that the cabinet might open. She wasn't ready to face Genie yet.

Genie sat quietly within. She knew Elinor wasn't alone. Still unsure as to whether Elinor had plans to destroy her home, she decided to bide her time. She would listen in to their conversation instead.

On the way home in her car, Elinor and Delia decided that they would act as normally as they could at the cottage. No talking of Jim, no mentioning of Vihaan and Gertrude. The genie wouldn't know where Elinor had been, and she would give the impression that she had met Delia off the plane. Elinor opened the bottle of wine, filled the two glasses, and sat down opposite Delia.

"I was delighted when you rang and asked if you could have a holiday break here, too bad your flight got delayed though. You would have been here yesterday otherwise."

"Yes, sorry about that. You ended up booking into a Premier inn?" Delia asked, keeping up the pretence.

"Oh, don't apologise. It didn't make sense to drive back home and then back out to the airport. You are here now and tomorrow we can have a quiet day on the beach. The water is still a bit cold for swimming, but okay for paddling along the shoreline." Elinor sighed. "I love this place, am so glad I found it last year. It's peaceful and the sea is right on my doorstep."

"When you described the cottage and your new purchase, I couldn't wait to see both." Delia gave a pretend sigh. "I need a few days away, my boss is driving me mad. Nothing I do is good enough. I need to find another job. You don't need an assistant, perchance? Help you to source the antiques on your list?" Delia winked. "Which reminds me, I brought you a gift. I saw it a while ago and thought of you." Delia gave Elinor a broad smile.

"Ooh, a present? For me? Thanks ever so much. What is it?" asked Elinor, playing along.

"Now, that would be telling, wouldn't it? I'll give it to you tomorrow, it's in my backpack, somewhere," Delia was trying hard not to burst into a fit of giggles.

"I can't wait to see it," teased Elinor. "Anyway, enjoy the wine, and your stay. The sea air will do you good."

Elinor refilled their glasses. The Amazon delivery was due tomorrow and she had requested that the driver stops at the gate leading down her road. She didn't want the driver to see Jim's car and needed to hide the package in the garage. Could djinns smell iron, she pondered.

The following morning, Elinor was up early. A text message had informed her that her package was due between 9 – 10 am. Not wanting to miss the driver, she made herself a mug of coffee and walked up the road to the gate. She saw Jim's car as she left, down by the beach wall. She still didn't know what to do about it. As she stood by the gate, keeping an eye out for the delivery van, she sipped her hot coffee. About twenty minutes later, she saw the van and held her hand up. A lot of the delivery vans drove straight past her turning, as the 'No through road' sign plus the 'No Entry' sign, put them off. He stopped the van and opened his door. Going around to the side of the vehicle, he opened the door and rummaged around for her box. A few moments later he was handing it over, got back in his van, and with a wave, drove off. Elinor walked back towards her cottage. Pressing the remote for the garage door, she entered her garage and set about opening the box. Inside, was a tall plastic container containing the iron filings. She knew there was a jar of PVA glue on one of the shelves, so stood the container next to it. With Delia's funnel, they were all set. She left the garage and pressed the remote to lock it. Feeling very happy with herself, she opened the door to her cottage and went back in. Taking her empty mug back to the kitchen, she washed it out and filled the kettle.

Whilst the kettle was heating up, Elinor headed up the stairs to give Delia a call. The bedroom door was open and Elinor could hear the shower running. She came back down the stairs, went back to the kitchen, and set out another mug.

Not long after, Delia walked into the hall, still drying her dark shoulder length hair. She stopped in the hall to admire the antique clock. Made out of dark mahogany wood, its pendulum swung from side to side. It had a square clock face. The numerals were Roman, and the clock hands were made of ornate brass. She waited for the hour hand to land on the ten. There were only seconds to wait. The clock started to chime. At the side of the clock, below the clock face, a brass plate slid out holding two figurines that stood opposite each other. As the plate stopped in the middle of the clock, the two figurines bowed to each other and then straightened back up as the plate slid back into the clock.

"Oh, wow! Just wow," said Delia, turning to see Elinor standing not far from her. "Where did you find that beauty? I'm so jealous."

Elinor beamed. "You wouldn't believe me, honestly," and laughed.

"Try me."

"Oh, OK then….it was eBay," seeing the look on Delia's face, she added, "I did, really," still laughing.

"No wonder the cabinet seems to like this spot in the hall. It's right underneath an amazing antique. I will be back at eleven to watch it again," grinned Delia. She turned towards Elinor and followed her to the kitchen.

Genie was feeling nosey. Who was this Delia? And why did her voice seem familiar? Genie was sure she had heard that voice, somewhere before. Well, that did explain Elinor's absence, and as she hadn't told her friend the truth about the cabinet, neither could she say what had happened to Jim. But….who was Delia?? Genie drew her knees up and rested her hands under her chin.

Delia and Elinor took their coffees outside and sat on the top steps that led to the beach. Delia sighed as she took in the view and sipped her coffee. As the steps weren't very wide, Elinor was sat on the next step down from Delia. She turned to look at her. "Are you OK?"

"Yes, am fine. Just thinking how lucky you are to live here. It's so quiet, even the sea is whispering," she gave another sigh. Lowering her voice, she continued, "No wonder you don't want your guest, though thinking about what I told you earlier, maybe it is just as well you didn't need any wishes—," Delia paused. Elinor nodded. She understood exactly what Delia didn't want to voice aloud. Elinor didn't know the genie's hearing range, guessed that Delia was thinking the same.

"Do you think she will show herself whilst I'm here?" whispered Delia.

"I don't know, but hopefully, curiosity will win the day. She must be wondering who you are," Elinor whispered back.

After they had drunk their coffee, dumping their mugs on the steps, they walked down to the beach, leaving their flip-flops on the bottom step.

Elinor was reminded of the last time she was here when Jim had startled her. She tried her best not to cry, but a shuddering sob escaped nevertheless. Delia put her arm around Elinor's shoulders.

"It's okay. When we get back I will give you your 'present,' which you can open whilst I'm watching your amazing clock. With any luck, it will pique the genie's curiosity enough to entice her out of the cabinet," soothed Delia.

Elinor gave her a weak smile. "Come on, I will race you to the water," tongue in cheek, as the tide was in and not far from their feet.

Just before the clock was due to chime in the eleventh hour, Delia went upstairs to the guest room and took the lamp out of her backpack. She had put it in a box and wrapped ribbon around it. She came back down and walking down the hall, stopped by the cabinet. She couldn't stop herself. Running her fingers along the top of the lid, she caressed the carvings. In the sunlight, the furniture glowed, the rosewood warm beneath her fingertips. Elinor joined her and stood beside her.

"It looks different every time I look at it, and the carvings are exquisite." Giving the gift to Elinor, she said, "Here you are, my friend, you can open it now. I hope you like it," giving Elinor a cheeky grin.

"Ooh, thank you. You wrapped this so beautifully, it seems a shame to open it."

Delia gave Elinor a prod. "Come on, open it…I want to see your reaction. I know your love of antiques, and I just couldn't resist it when I saw it."

Genie listened to their repartee and wondered herself what Delia was giving Elinor. She was dying to open the lid and have a peek, but with them both standing right in front…

Elinor untied the ribbon, opened the box, and squealed in delight.

"Oh my god, where did you find this? I've wanted one for years. There are a lot of imitations around, but this! Oooh, it's the real McCoy."

Genie was getting impatient…

"Hmm, you don't like it then?" teased Delia. "I can take it back if you like." A Cheshire cat grin across her features.

"Oh no you don't. Hands off. It's mine. I want it, am keeping it!"

The clock started to chime and drowned out what Elinor said next, probably because she whispered it. Genie strained her ears, but could only hear the clock as it struck the chimes, then there was a whirring sound as the brass plate emerged from the clock, and at that moment they both heard the click of the lock. Elinor nudged Delia.

The lid slowly opened…

"Look, Elinor, the cabinet is opening. Has that happened before?" as Delia nudged Elinor back.

She didn't get a chance to reply, as a mist swirled up out of the cabinet.

Delia, even though she knew there was a genie in the cabinet, nevertheless, was stunned. As the mist swirled and spun, a face started to emerge; two bright blue eyes fixed on the object in Elinor's hands. The eyes blinked and widened. A pink rosebud mouth appeared below the eyes and was shaped into an O.

Delia fainted.

When Delia came around, she opened her eyes and got back to her feet, albeit unsteadily.

"Are you alright, Delia? You gave me a shock," asked Elinor, as her friend was still looking pale.

Delia looked at the genie wide-eyed. "Uh, yes, I just wasn't expecting..." leaving the sentence unfinished.

Genie was sat on the cabinet with her legs crossed and barefooted. She was dressed as before; holding the brass lamp, studying it with her blue eyes wide open.

"Delia," Genie lifted her head. "How lovely to see you, and what a beautiful gift you have given Elinor." The djinn slowly caressed the lamp, which gleamed under her touch.

"Uh," stuttered Delia. "Oh my, you are gorgeous. Rupert always said that there was a djinn with long blonde hair. Oh, I wouldn't rub that if I were you."

"Oh? Why not?" replied the genie. "I think it is quite tactile." She lifted the stopper on the top of the lamp that was attached to a chain. "And, is this where the oil goes in?" Delia was struggling to speak, so Elinor spoke up.

"Yes, Genie. Delia said not to rub the lamp because another, um," Elinor paused, not sure how to word it without causing offence. Genie looked up.

"Ah, another one like me, perhaps? Is that what you meant?"

Delia found her voice. "Yes, that is what we meant."

"But, Delia, you could have your own genie, if that was the case. I expect you have lots of wishes that need granting." Genie looked at Delia with a penetrating stare, her mouth spread into a wide, mean smile.

"Um, actually, am okay thanks," Delia replied, her voice betraying a feeling of unease. She understood now why Elinor felt so frightened of her unwanted guest.

"Oh, come now Delia. You aren't happy with your job, your life in general. I think you could do with a few wishes being granted. Don't you agree, Elinor?"

Elinor didn't like the way this conversation was going and thought hard about what to reply. She didn't want to goad the genie into something that could go horribly wrong.

"Well," Elinor paused as she thought about how to continue. "Is there a way of finding out, without rubbing the lamp?" Elinor mentally crossed her fingers. Would the djinn take the bait?

"Hmm, let's see," the genie continued, studying the lamp. "I suppose I could have a peek inside."

"Oh, um, I wouldn't advise that," spoke up Elinor, trying to ignore the hard stare she got from Delia. "Um, what I mean is, what if there is, um, something in there? Couldn't it hurt you?" Elinor hoping that this would work.

"Isn't that what you want though, Elinor?" Genie regarded her with a penetrating stare. "To be rid of me?"

"Well, you see Genie. After I left to pick up Delia from the airport and realised that due to fog, her flight had been delayed, I took the opportunity to stay in a hotel and have a think about my life. You are right, I don't need anyone else. I have you for company, plus anything my heart desires. So, I would like you to stay." Elinor double-crossed her fingers, metaphorically, hoping that she had managed to put enough sincerity into her passionate speech.

Delia, realising what Elinor was doing, chipped in with, "Ah, Elinor does have a point there. I mean, she is so lucky to have her very own djinn."

Genie regarded the two women, not sure if they were being honest with her. She needed to think about it. Handing the lamp back to Elinor, she said, "I will be back later." With that she rose up into a swirling mist, the cabinet lid opened and she swooped back inside.

Elinor looked at Delia and put her finger on her mouth. Now was not the time or place to discuss what had just happened.

"Are you hungry, Delia? There is a lovely bistro not far from here. We can have some lunch and a walk along the promenade after.

****

By 12.30 pm they were both at a bistro, further along the promenade than the one Jim and Elinor had been to. It had been a silent car journey, both women contemplating the recent events. Elinor had put the lamp in her tote bag, along with her mobile, purse, and car keys. She had also added the iron filings to her bag.

Delia had raised her eyebrows when she saw the plastic container being added to the tote bag. Elinor had just grimaced and said, "Tell you later."

They ordered their food and drinks, and now that Elinor felt safe to talk, she chatted to Delia.

"OK, I hope we are far enough away to talk without ears hearing us. I put that container in my bag," Elinor being cautious about what she said. "Because I am sure that the djinn looks around my cottage in my absence. I don't want her seeing it if she goes into the garage. I brought the lamp with me so that she doesn't do what we want her to do, whilst we are out."

Delia regarded Elinor with solemn eyes. "I owe you an apology. I hadn't realised how scary that thing is. No wonder you are frightened, let alone what else she has done to you. I couldn't believe my eyes when that lid rose. I know you said she was in there, but, even so, she frightened the life out of me! I have never fainted before."

Elinor put her hand on Delia's. "I know we

haven't known each other for long, but I hope that we will remain friends after this is over. I fully understand what you are saying, in your shoes, I'd have probably thought the same. I don't think even your uncle realises what scary shits the djinns are."

Delia gave a rueful laugh. "I certainly will be telling him. No wonder he is obsessed with them, but, I am sure he has never met one. We talk about djinns and we know they are spiteful and mean, but they also mess with your head. I could almost feel her listening to my thoughts as I spoke. She knew all my fears and doubts, thank god she didn't realise that I don't have a boss though. You knew she would be listening to us talking and when she said my name….my blood ran cold," Delia shuddered. "I feel for Arjun now. I didn't before. I mean I was sympathetic, but, jeez, when that djinn gave me that mean smile after saying I could do with a genie…my god, I thought I was going to faint again."

Elinor looked up as their food and drinks arrived. In a way, she was pleased that Delia was afraid of Genie. It would make the next part much easier now that she realised what they were dealing with.

Genie sat in the cabinet, deep in thought. She was sure that something was going on, but couldn't place her finger on it and neither could she remember where she had seen or heard Delia, and that was bothering her. When she thought of the lamp though, her eyes lit up. How she coveted it. She needed to think how she could get it off Elinor, who obviously loved it.

After they had eaten and were drinking coffee, Elinor remarked that a walk along the promenade would clear the cobwebs. Delia was inclined to agree. Since her encounter with the djinn, she had felt distinctly unwell. Sick to the stomach really, with fear. She was beginning to regret agreeing to this. She wasn't about to let Elinor down though. They had to work out the next plan of action and realised that Elinor had been right when she had placed doubt in the mind of the djinn.

"I'm sure that your genie wants the lamp," remarked Delia, as they walked along the promenade eating ice cream.

"I was working towards that. I saw how her eyes lit up when she saw it. You'd fainted, so missed her taking it from me."

"I did see how she was caressing it though, her face when she was thinking of looking inside it, I could have hit you when you advised her against it, but then I could see what you were doing. Clever you."

"She will do what she thinks we don't want her to do, plus, we know she covets the lamp. I'm sure that when we get back, she will be sitting on the cabinet, waiting for us. Eager to get her hands on it again."

"So, how do we play this now? Give her the lamp and see what she does? I have a feeling that she will pop inside it and have look, intending to say that there is something inside and that she should keep it."

"Yes, that's what I think as well, so have that

stopper ready. I wonder if we should try to dissuade her one more time. I want her determined to look inside it." Elinor finished her ice cream.

"Let's play it by ear, it has worked so far. And now that I understand your thinking, I will just follow your lead." Delia laughed. "It was supposed to be me that was the distraction, but it has worked out to be the lamp itself."

"Oh, I definitely needed you. This would not have worked without you. The djinn was dying of curiosity regarding the present from you. You were brilliant! Even I was excited and I knew what you were giving me!" Elinor turned towards Delia and hugged her.

****

An hour later, Elinor was pulling up outside her garage, she opened the door and drove inside. Once out of the car, Delia removed the silver funnel and the bung from her handbag. Walking over to the shelf, she picked up the jar of PVA glue and opened it, whilst Elinor got the container of filings and removed the lid. She handed Delia a small paint brush to apply the glue. Delia put the brush into the glue and lightly coated the bung, then dipped it into the container, putting it back on the shelf to dry. Doing the same with the funnel stem, she put that back on the shelf. Picking up the bung, they both left the garage and Elinor locked it.

"This should be interesting, what do you reckon?" she asked as they approached the cottage.

Delia hesitated.

"What's next?" she hissed to Elinor.

"Stay calm, I'm sure she will be waiting for us."

Elinor unlocked her front door; butterflies were dancing in her stomach. Delia followed her in. Sure enough, Genie was sat on the cabinet patiently waiting. Having thought about the situation, she had decided that the best way to get the lamp off Elinor, was by telling her that there was something inside it, something so awful it needed to be destroyed, and, of course, she could deal with that.

"Hello Elinor, Delia," chirped Genie, as they came in through the door. Do you have the lamp, Elinor? I couldn't see it around anywhere." Thus confirming Elinor's suspicions of earlier.

"Yes, I have it with me. I couldn't bear to leave it behind. I have wanted one of these lamps for so long, I have only ever come across imitations. Why?"

"Oh, well, thinking about it, I decided that perhaps I should take a peek inside it. I wouldn't want any harm to come to you, my dear." Genie smiled at Elinor with her big blue eyes.

"That's ok, I'm sure that nothing is hiding in it. Besides, we wouldn't want anything to happen to you either. As I said earlier, you are great company for me. What would I do without you?" Elinor answered, hoping that the djinn would be insistent.

"Oh, don't worry about me, I can handle myself. Let me have the lamp, I mean, let me have a look at the lamp," the djinn now starting to realise that this wasn't going to be as easy as she thought.

"What do you reckon, Delia?" asked Elinor, trying hard not to grin. "Do you think there is anything to worry about?"

"Not at all, but there again, if your djinn is concerned for your welfare...I suppose it couldn't do any harm, her having a look? I mean, an intensive search inside would alleviate any fears that we may have...but, no Elinor, you're right. Nothing to be worried about. Shall we go to the beach?" Delia turned towards the front door. Elinor was about to do the same, following Delia's lead.

"Well, I'm not so sure. When I was holding it earlier, I'm positive I could, hmm, feel something inside it. I would be a lot happier if you would just let me have a peek, or even a good look inside as Delia suggested. You could leave it with me whilst you go off to the beach." Genie looked at them both, her blue eyes giving nothing away.

Elinor turned back towards the djinn. "Oh, go on then. I suppose you are looking after my best interests." She dug around in her tote bag and slowly brought out the lamp. Turning it in her hands, she reluctantly went to pass it to the genie. The djinn tried to grab it, but Elinor quickly retracted her hand.

"Just a minute, I want to watch what you're doing, no taking it back into the cabinet with you, I might not see it again."

"That's okay, Elinor. You put it on the cabinet and I will swoop inside. It won't take a second. If I find anything ominous, I will pop right back out and tell you." Genie was feeling excited. The lamp would be hers, come what may!

Elinor put the lamp on the top of the cabinet. Genie did what she promised; swirling up into a mist, she flew into the lamp using the spout. As quick as a flash, Delia used the bung to prevent her from escaping and held on to the top with the chain for dear life.

"Now what?" hissed Delia, who was shaking with fear; God help them both if the djinn managed to escape.

"Keep calm and pass it to me. There is iron on the stopper remember, we did both, the funnel and the bung."

As Elinor held the lamp, she could feel it vibrating. Genie, as soon as she had entered through the spout, realised, too late, that she had fallen into a trap. So eager had she been to have the lamp for herself, hadn't seen it coming. As she tried to fly back out, the iron on the stopper burned her. She screamed and flung her misty form around the inside of the lamp. Elinor looked at Delia, "I don't think we need the funnel, the iron on the stopper might be enough."

They both listened to the screaming coming from within the vessel that the genie was trapped in. Eventually, all went silent, the lamp stopped vibrating. They both felt guilty, causing the djinn to die—but, it had to be this way.

****

Elinor placed the lamp onto the cabinet. The lid

was closed and locked.

"Do you think the cabinet will reopen its lid again at some point? You said that it seemed to be a separate entity from the djinn. Could it yield yet more secrets?" Delia questioned Elinor, who had been contemplating the same. She also asked herself if Jim was going to return.

"I don't know, it's a scary scenario. However, its feet are still embedded into my floor, so it doesn't look like it is going to go away anytime soon."

"What should we do with the lamp? Are we sure that your genie is dead?" Delia was still looking pale. She shuddered as she thought of what the consequences might be if the djinn was just injured and lying quiet; waiting for someone to remove the top so that she could escape.

It was at this point that they heard the knocker rat-a-tat on the wooden door of the cottage. Elinor opened the door with trepidation. A handsome man, with grey eyes, an aquiline nose, and a generous mouth smiled at her.

"JIM!" Elinor shouted as she let him in. Delia looked at him in astonishment; her face paled even more, as she passed out in a dead faint.

THE END